FROM KINDERGARTEN TO 12TH GRADE CAN = 13 YEARS A SLAVE

Rickie Clark

Copyright@ 2019 Rickie Clark

All rights reserved.

ISBN: 978-1092523028

FORWARD

I began writing this book in 2016, during the time that Hillary Clinton submitted her name as a presidential candidate. During this time, I would ask this question to just about everyone I encountered such as friends, my family members, co-workers, or people I would meet randomly. I would ask people that I met at various conferences, workshops, community and city council meetings, and even in barbershops.

The question I posed was, "Can you think of any book, from kindergarten to twelfth grade, that was a required reading, that speaks positively about people of color?"

Then I would follow the previous question with another one. "If you were an alien and you came to America and studied from kindergarten to twelfth grade what would you think of people of color, particularly Africans?

Would you believe the history told to us from kindergarten to 12th grade!? And for the life of me, I can't understand why they label us an angry people, when they began slavery in 1619. Their history of us began in 1619, but our history began in Africa in a state of freedom.

African history started in Africa and that is relatively understandable. Yet, African-American history started here in America. More importantly, it changed America and was an integral part of U.S. history. African American history played a major part in its buildings, roads, cities states and policies. African American history navigated the way for women's rights, human rights, civil rights, gay rights and the rights for the disabled. The laws that prevent discrimination based on race, creed, religion, sexual orientation and skin color that Caucasian women, Hispanics, and other minorities benefit from; happened, because of African Americans. Just about every book I read from K-12 through college seemed to be a negative read pertaining to people of color. I can't speak for everyone else who went to school in America but I can honestly say, that when I attended school from K-12th grade I was disappointed because everything I knew about Africa and African people was negative.

Then, I attended Jarvis Christian College, which was an all-Black college, or as they are called, HBCUs (Historical Black Colleges and Universities). There weren't any textbooks, or required readings that were positively centered about people of color there.

Every book pertaining to people of color would begin "my history" in 1619, which happens to be the beginning of slavery. Not one book in the entire school library and I'm including college and high school, not one book in the "lie bury," where they buried the lies, spoke positive about people of color; especially "Africans."

I've heard some people make comments like, "Oh I know a good book." They would go on to ask, "do you know the titles, *I Know Why the Caged Bird Sings*, *Native Son* or the *Color Purple*?'

I wound eagerly respond, are any of those books about something positive?

They would reply, "they made it through the struggle." Then they would come back with, "Rick, what about him? You know, the one that made things out of the peanut?"

"I would say, "you're talking about the one or two pages or a paragraph about George Washington Carver?"

Think about it, when Carver invented those items out of peanuts it was during the Jim Crow era. Some people would say, "what about the man who made the gas mask and the stop light?"

I would say, "you're talking about Garrett Morgan." Again, that was during the Jim Crow separate but equal era, again nothing positive about people of color, especially, African Americans. Just about everything that speaks of Africans in the educational system has never spoken positively about people of color, especially Africans, not even in the Museums of Natural History, Science & Industry, or Technology of Art. If these places do have something positive, it's just like our books, very little; maybe one page, one paragraph or there is a page in a book or one section in the museums.

It's been stated that slaves were taken from Africa and brought to America. This is not true, people were taken from Africa and made into slaves. Marcus Garvey said, "*Over 400 years ago our ancestors were taken from the great continent of Africa and brought here for the purpose of using them as slaves. Without mercy, without sympathy, they worked our fore fathers, they suffered, they bled and they died, but they had a hope that one day their young would be free.*"

My question is, where is that freedom? Are we free-dom? Are 'N's made in America or did integration work? The information that we read on a daily basis seems to indicate that we are either still slaves or indentured servants.

Here in America we go to school approximately 20,000 hrs from K-12. That's a lot of time to encourage and remind students of color of their value or lack thereof. In that much time you can either educate or mis-educate. I think we have done the latter. Because from kindergarten to 12th grade, can equal 13 years a slave.

Dedication

This writing is being dedicated to my ancestors and my grandchildren. As they have been my inspiration for this writing. For the fact that my grandchildren will have to grow up in this education system, not ever knowing that their ancestors have designed pyramids that sit in the center of the earth. Also, that it was their ancestors that taught Plato, Pythagoras and Socrates; who mistakenly thought that the earth was flat. They(my ancestors) knew that the earth was round. I say to my grandchildren, **"build young people, build!"**

My Ancestors: George Washington Grace-great-great-grandfather; Georgia Grace Overton-Great Grandmother; James Overton-Great Grandfather; Odell Datus Davis-Grandfather; Fannie Mae Davis-Grandmother; Melissa Whitfield-Rich-Great Grandmother; Eddie V McNeal-Grandfather; Mary Lou McNeal-Grandmother; Manuel McNeal-father; Wenfret Davis (Winnie)-mother; Cecil Davis-Uncle; Chester Walker-Uncle; Magnolia(Bunny) Dallas-Auntie; Dorothy Fife-Auntie; Kathryn Key-Auntie; Alfred Davis-Uncle; Charles Walker-Cousin; Jeffrey Dallas-Cousin; Derrick Key-cousin; Manuel McNeal-Brother; Bernard Walker-Cousin; Craig Key-Cousin; George Fife-Cousin; David Branch Jr.-Cousin.
My Grandchildren: Amber, Ashley, Ri-Ri, Rikkia, Rikki Jr., and Rihyann

If I left a name out, charge it to my head; not to my heart.

Special Acknowledgments of Contributors

Dr. James Branch, Jr

Pharoah Davis

Tony D. Hudson

Minister Lee Muhammed

Amin Imau Ojuok

JaCinto Ramos

Amon Rashidi

Rickie Clark

Introduction

Growing up, I learned very little about our history. By the time I started school, I vividly remember not even caring. By the time I was six years old, all my super heroes were white. Superman, Batman, Aquaman, and even Birdman were all muscle bound white men that saved the world from destruction every day. At home, I ate dinner underneath a picture of the Last Supper, 13 white men, including one that was the Son of God. The only Africans I saw, and I mean this literally, before I entered the 1st grade, were the ones that Tarzan beat up every Saturday morning on Channel 11. And I was NOT one of them. It was obvious, at least to me, that I was Tarzan because I stood for what Tarzan stood for: justice.

As I got older, 98% of all the males that I saw fight for justice were white. I knew that Dr. King fought for justice, but he got shot. Bullets bounced right off of Superman. Every time I learned about a black person that fought for justice, either they never achieved it, or they achieved it through the benevolence and superior power of white people. Black super heroes were always weaker than Superman and not as smart as Batman. By the time I entered 3rd grade, I was already indoctrinated with white supremacy. By the time I was in the 5th grade, I knew, and could verbalize, that God was white, Adam and Eve were white, and that black people came from white people that stayed out in the sun too long. I knew that we came from slaves; not from Africa, but from slaves.

By the time I reached high school, not only did I understand that we came from slaves, I could articulate how, even though slavery was bad, at least we ended up in America. At least we learned how to worship Jesus. I remember being especially grateful that we were "rescued" from Africa! While I had grown fond of learning "Black History" (the story of Black people in America), I had zero interest in African History, primarily because I was sure it didn't exist. I remember being fascinated with Dr. King, Rosa Parks, Harriet Tubman, and Jackie Robinson. I remember my anger and disappointment in the 11th grade, when my U.S. History teacher, Mr. Hill (Rest in Power), assigned me a little, dark skinned man named Marcus Garvey as the subject of my term paper. Who was Marcus Garvey? Upon doing research, and finding out that Mr. Garvey wanted Black people to go "back to Africa", I became immediately disinterested in the paper and the Black man that taught such nonsense. Why would we go back to the jungle? Didn't Garvey know that Africa was full of cannibals and savages that would eat us? Furthermore, didn't Garvey realize that we can't do anything without White people? After all, we were called Afro-American and/or African American because of our hair texture, right?

    I had been, and my peers had been, "mis-educated". We'd been led to believe that our story began with slavery and that the same institution that kidnapped us; civilized us. We'd been taught that inclusion was the mission and acceptance was the goal.
I was invited to speak at a school awards ceremony. I gave a speech entitled, *Why Didn't I Learn this Sooner?* I made a heartfelt and honest appeal to faculty, staff, and parents to cease and desist the mis-education of Black children. While I'm sure the majority of the

audience hadn't learned our history, I'm just as sure that everyone knew what I was talking about. Everyone knew that our history was being hidden from us. No one enjoyed beginning their story with slavery. Slavery is not African History. Slavery is an interruption of African History that lasted for fewer years than Kemet's golden ages, Mali's dominance of West African trade, the Moorish occupation of Spain, and Great Zimbabwe's architectural revolution.

When I attended K - 12 school, I was identified one of seven ways: nigger, negro, colored, black, African-American, American or African. By the time I finished high school I knew that I was three things: a Black man(when we talked about race), an African American(when we talked about ethnicity), and a nigga(when we talked about everything else).

The struggles that those who came before us went through, built their successes, even though there were failures along the way. Through history we learn about various approaches to warfare and battle strategy and diplomacy. We learn that people haven't changed, but their customs, religions and values have.

We also learn about the accomplishments of humans as a whole as well as on an individual level. We learn about the environment these people grew up in and how it contributed to the inventions they made.

Finally, we learn how those values, customs, wars and inventions molded the past generations and how they continue to mold us today. The problem with hiding a race's history, which has been done to African descendent people for centuries now; is that we all lose a piece of the puzzle that is needed to properly interpret the historical clues left behind. When history gets white-washed, it clouds and muddies the glass that we all look through for information. We've all heard the phrase "when you tell one lie, it leads to another." Well, when you're dealing with historic events, this can become a serious problem for obvious reasons. This is why African history is important. Because without all of it (the unfiltered, untarnished, un-tampered truth), we don't really understand our past. And understanding our past is key to understanding ourselves. Scientists work hard to base everything they do off the facts that they know. They use this knowledge to make important discoveries that we all benefit from. They don't make up facts because they understand the ripple effect it will cause. Historians owe it to the world, to do the same. It wasn't until Africans started reclaiming their history that they found out just how white-washed things had become. Let's just say that these lies aren't helping anyone, they just make history less clear and unobtainable to those who are trying to find the truth. But African-American history is important because that field of study dispels a lot of the lies and seeks to give us back the knowledge that was taken from us.

Rickie Clark

TABLE OF CONTENTS

Forward 2

Dedication 6

Introduction 8

CHAPTER 1 - Educate Me About What? 13

CHAPTER 2 - Are We Free-Dumb? 19

CHAPTER 3 - Did Integration Work? 25

CHAPTER 4 - The Miss-Education of the No-Grow 31

CHAPTER 5 - To Give Back or Go Back? 37

CHAPTER 6 - N's Are Only Made In America 48

CHAPTER 7 - Racial Equity Walk 55

APPENDIX

    Racial Biographies 61

    Appendix A - 50 African History Questions 89

    Appendix B - Recommended Readings 92

    Appendix C - Recommended Movies 96

    Appendix D - Recommended Documentaries 97

    Appendix E - 50 Questions Answer Key 98

    About The Author 101

    How to Work With Rickie Clark 102

CHAPTER 1
Educate Me About What?

It was Malcolm X who said, "Education is the passport to the future, for tomorrow belongs to the people who prepare for it today." Now I have the utmost respect for Malcolm X. Though I often wonder what education and whose education. When I look up the word education it states: the knowledge, skill, and understanding that you get from attending a school, college, or university. My question is, 'knowledge of what, skills to work for whom, and a understanding that you are less than and not equal to.'

I believe that education is more than reading; more than writing, it's more than math. It must also, teach you who you are. To me, educating(knowledge and skills) Africans from Kindergarten to 12th grade in this system, teaches us that African people are taught to serve and white people are taught to rule. They teach Africans about other peoples' civilizations, but teaches us about individuals, i.e., Martin Luther King, Malcolm X, George Washington Carver and the list goes on. If you can't see the racism in that, then surely, we have a problem. Look at the information they give us about people of color, especially black people and what are we being trained to do?

When I think about the education (knowledge and skills) or the lack thereof that I received here, in this, yet to be, United States of America what knowledge and skills am I being given? As a person of color, what am I being trained to do, for whom and for what?

The word education comes from the Latin word educe. Which means to bring out (as something latent). Better educe implies the bringing out of something potential or latent <*educed* order out of chaos>.

As African's we must clean our minds of all the negative information and beliefs that have been given to us, about our people and ourselves. We must educe, pull out what's good. We have no other choice. When it comes to the mis-education here in America, we must either destroy it or accept African inferiority.

I have come to the realization that educated people are taught to do for self, trained people are taught to do for others. Which one are we? I think we are trained, not educated. How is it that we have more money now, yet, we own less land than we did post slavery and we have less home ownership.

But we claim to be educated, talking about we have BS, MS and PHDs; yet our communities and our children are suffering from a lack of educe. When your oppressor controls what you think about yourself, he needs no chains or walls to control you. It was Carter G. Woodson who said, "If you control a persons thinking, you don't have to worry about his actions." So again, I ask the question, "Educate me about what?"

One problem that we face as African Americans is the importance of higher learning about self. For example, The Bureau of Labor Statistics (2013) stated that, 3.2 million youth graduated from high school in 2011-2012. From this statistic, 66.2% subsequently enrolled in colleges or universities. Moreover, community colleges enrolled nearly half of the students in public undergraduate programs and a disproportionate number of first-generation, low-income, under-prepared, and minority students. The national completion agenda initiated by President Barack Obama had brought both visibility and pressure to community colleges; which had completion rates of less than 25% for first-time and full-time students. African-American students rates were even lower than part-time students. When comparing four-year traditional collegiate institutions with community colleges, more African-American males had enrolled into community colleges because of open admission policies, a variety of program offerings, and convenient locations.

On the other hand, community colleges were more likely to lose these students because of employment, leniency within admission policies, and personal challenges. African-American male inclusion into postsecondary educational opportunities has become a topic of national policy and priority within the nation. For example, President Barack Obama challenged the nation in a "State of the Union" address to regain its status as the global leader with the highest proportion of postsecondary graduates in the world by 2025. Therefore, increasing the number of college graduates who possess skills and technical knowledge needed to compete in an increasingly advanced economy. This would sustain the country's positioning as a global force, secure the nation's homeland, and improve future science and technology innovations. According to the National Center for Education Statistics (NCES, 2012), African-American male students performed significantly below other ethnicities in all areas. College graduation rates among African-American males do not equal the graduation rates compared to other ethnicities and genders.

So again I ask, "Educate me about what?"

Notes

Rickie Clark

Quote

"Africa is the Mother of civilization and the land where the very foundation in socialization practices was laid."
~Asa G. Hillard, III

CHAPTER 2
Are We Free-Dumb?

      I believe that Freedom and Liberty go hand in hand. When you have true freedom you are liberated to think for self and do for self. And it's been stated that it's only when you begin your history in your state of freedom that you can come to properly understand your role in life.

      All Africans born in America, who begin their history in 1619, will never solve our people's problems. In order to solve our people's problems we must begin our history in freedom. And when I say Freedom, I'm not talking about free and dumb.
Think about it, we're the only people who begin our history, in slavery. If we begin our history in slavery, the best we can do is become a better Slave. Name a time when black people were not enslaved but empowered? I always get the same answer, 'I can't think of one.' So, if we can't describe freedom, and don't know what it

looks like. How do we know when we are free? Then the sad part is, how do we explain it to our children and our children's children. Are they to come into this world and be subservient because we are free and dumb? We can't lead where we don't go. And we can't teach what we don't know.

Images shape our reality, and if we haven't seen greatness, how do you strive for greatness? If you haven't seen Freedom how do you strive for freedom? Because if you don't know what it was, you can't know what it is. If you don't know what it is, then you are ill prepared for what is to come.

Now that's scary because we have been living here in this yet to be, United States of America, for over 400 years, in a subservient role or better yet as second-class citizens. Therefore, if we as a people don't know how Freedom looks, we don't know what it's like to be in charge. We don't know what it's like, to run our own states, countries, or continents. Then we will do just like our ancestors did, during the Emancipation Proclamation; go back to 'Massa' for work.

Take a look at South Africa, they realize that Apartheid(apart-hate) was wrong and you and I, realize Apartheid was wrong. So they ended Apartheid, but the Europeans continue to own everything they stole. The gold mines, diamond mines and the best part of the land in South Africa. Is that what Freedom looks like? Yes, we protest, to sit on the bus, but we don't own it. We fought to live in their neighborhoods, but we don't own them. We protest to sit at your restaurant to eat but we don't own the restaurants. And last but not least, we fought and protested to get into your schools, colleges, and universities. Only to learn European history that clearly degrades people of African dissent. Remember people that don't treat you right, don't teach you right. Hear me when I say, "what you study most, is what you love most." Keep in mind we have had emancipation, Jim Crowe, Separate but equal Civil Rights and Apartheid but never Freedom. Or are we Free-Dumb?

If you celebrate the defeat of your enemy over you, then you are a fool!! That's the question Fredrick Douglass asked during a speech in Rochester, New York, on July 5, 1852. That speech titled, "The Meaning of July 4th to the Negro," is among Douglass' most famous public addresses in part because it focuses on the irony of a country celebrating its freedom while holding millions of people in bondage.

But there's another reason why Douglass' words still resonate 150 years later. It's that his fundamental question still remains. How are black people in America, still mired in institutional racism created by slavery and white supremacy, supposed to celebrate their country? By no stretch of the imagination are black people still slaves in America. But the institutions created by slavery, namely white supremacy, still dictate black lives daily. Nowhere is this reality as stark today than in our criminal justice system.

There are degrees of freedom. If we define "freedom" as "as free as the average white person," then the answer is simple: Hell no. Obviously, opinions vary among black people, but the majority of opinions, I'd say, exist within a narrow range. While a subset of black Americans may build up the illusion of freedom by accumulating wealth, education, and/or power, try walking in a heavily patrolled black neighborhood, where the police stop and frisk black people with impunity. Try 'talking back' to a police officer or refusing to be searched. After that, tell me how "free" you are; that is if, you're still alive. Consider the large number of incarcerated black people in America unfree, by definition, which is greater than the number of black people who were enslaved in 1850, often for drug crimes (for which they may or may not be guilty). Though white people commit those same drug crimes at the same or greater rates, their incarceration rates are exceptionally low.

If and when people of color are released, they can't vote or get a job because of a felony conviction. I consider incarcerated people to be, in fact, people. So no, I'm going to say that black people don't feel free in America. Nor should they.

It's not an exaggeration to say that after over 400 years of this kind of oppression, an overwhelming amount of black people would be better off somehow moving to another country if they could.

Really, are we Free-Dumb?

Notes

Rickie Clark

Quote

"The history of Black Africa (and Black People) will remain suspended in air and cannot be written correctly until African historians dare to connect it with the history of Kemet/Egypt."
~ Cheikh Anta Diop

CHAPTER 3
Did Integration Work?

On May 17, 1954, the Supreme Court ruled, in the Brown v. Board of Education case, that segregated public schools were unconstitutional. Before the "Brown" decision, it was legal to have racially segregated public institutions and facilities as long as accommodations were equal in quality.

The government's failure to maintain and protect "equality in accommodation", for African Americans created an obvious gap in quality of life between the white and the black communities. While African Americans were paying taxes, they were not receiving public services near on par as whites. Segregated bathroom facilities, water fountains and most importantly, public schools were found to be deliberately sabotaged and underfunded by local and state governments that were determined to curtail and control the economic and political progress of the African American community, while maintaining a social hierarchy, rooted in the myth of white supremacy.

Black leaders argued that while African American families were paying their share into local and state coffers, not only were public accommodations not equal but black owned businesses were not receiving contracts to construct and provide those accommodations to the black community.

African Americans were terrorized at "negro polling stations" and denied the right to vote. Furthermore, African American educators had little or no control over school budgets, curriculum, hiring, and/or expansion of their own institutions. In many school districts, "colored schools", would be forced to use outdated and used supplies from white schools that were being "over-funded" meaning they were receiving the benefit of tax dollars from both communities.

Segregation is commonly defined as, "the separation of one group from another based on race or ethnicity". But segregation is not a synonym of separation. Segregation is, "separation with control". In other words it's the isolation or forced gathering of a particular group into a defined area of integration? According to Webster, to integrate is to, "blend while maintaining economic and political control of said group". To be perfectly honest, after slavery, and during Jim Crow, African Americans were not eager to live in close proximity with white people due to the inherent danger that would come with that scenario."

Many Black folk back then didn't mind the 'separate' they just wanted the 'equal'. Somehow, the narrative was shifted to, 'inclusion' rather than, 'equity'. The fight against 'segregation' became an emotional fight about Black "access" to traditionally white institutions on a consumer level, rather than an ownership level. For example, one of the great 'success stories' of the integration era is the Jackie Robinson saga.

Jackie is credited with "breaking the color barrier" in baseball, and is credited with being the first Black professional baseball player in US history. When the Brooklyn Dodgers signed Jackie, professional baseball was declared "integrated". The definition of integration is, "into a unified, functioning whole," or to "bring into equal membership in society or an organization." Jackie Robinson wasn't an isolated baseball player looking for an opportunity. He was already a professional baseball player in the Negro Leagues. Negro League baseball boasted about some of the greatest players the world has ever seen. It produced an entertaining brand of baseball that was not only thriving, but beginning to attract white fans. Jackie Robinson didn't represent "black baseball", the Negro League did. If the goal was to integrate baseball, wouldn't they have had to merge leagues, not just sign away one player? Touting Jackie Robinson as the 'first Black person to play professional baseball', looked like racial progress, socially, while devaluing a prominent African American institution; economically.

School integration had the same effect. While the narrative was focused on black students enrolling in white schools, black schools in many areas continued to be under funded, on top of now dealing with a decrease in enrollment. Over 60 years after Brown v. Board of Education we not only have to ask ourselves if integration worked, we have to ask ourselves if integration ever truly happened.

Did African American children become equal participants within the school system? Was there a "blending" of student bodies, institutional power, curriculum, and culture that resulted in a diverse learning environment that was beneficial to all involved? And what of historically black institutions? Was there an infusion of white students along with the enrollment dollars allotted to them, into the black community? For every African American professional that received an opportunity at a historically white institution, how many African Americans lost jobs, businesses, and opportunities as a result of the continued erosion of historically black institutions? What happened to the black owned corner store, the black owned taxi company, the black factory competing for contracts, and the middle class African American presence in the black community?

Finally, do African Americans control the economics and politics in the black community any more today than we did in the 1950s? It seems that while we were celebrating the 'integration of individuals', we ignored the further 'segregation' of our institutions.

Notes

Rickie Clark

Quote

"Many white Americans of good will have never connected bigotry with economic exploitation. They have deplored prejudice but tolerated or ignored economic injustice."
~Dr. Martin Luther King Jr.

Chapter 4
This Miss-Education of the No-Grow

Have you either heard of or know of the book entitled, *The Miss Education of the Negro* by Carter G. Woodson? This book was written in 1961 and the sad part is that it applies today. He calls us Negro and I'll call us No-Grow; No-Grow because we have not grown as a people since slavery, during slavery or after slavery.

Think about it, the same people who enslaved you, are now educating you, from their frame of reference, not your frame of reference. I believe if they don't treat you right, they can't teach you right. We are the only people who send our children to people other than ourselves to teach them. Cats don't send their kittens to dogs to teach them. Think about it. Every other race of people, except black people have their own educational institutions and every other institution; i.e., banks, hospitals, and lending organizations... but we as a people have to send our people to someone else for those services.

The sad part about this, it's like this all over the world. Name one black university owned and operated by black people that white people send their children to? I'll wait!

Let me see if I can help. Europeans send their children to European institutions. Asians send their children to Asian institutions. As a matter of fact the Jewish religion has a Jewish institution, and they send their children to Jewish institutions. Now don't get me wrong, they do attend other institutions, but they don't send their children to African, African-American or black institutions, in large numbers. Ask Morehouse, Howard, or Spelman.

As a matter of fact, some of our most brilliant, most intelligent young people throughout the world attend some of the most brilliant European institutions throughout the world. However, the most brilliant, most intelligent young Europeans, Asians, or people of India, don't attend the most brilliant black institutions, nowhere in the world.

But we as No-Grows are being educated by everybody else but ourselves. Then there's no wonder why we haven't grown. Remember what you study most, is what you love most.
You are probably asking what do I mean by that. I'm glad you asked. If you study European history from Kindergarten to 12th grade, then you will love the European culture.

Why? Because that's what you know, sometimes that's the only thing we know.

For some of us we are scared of the African culture. We view our motherland through the eyes of a European curriculum. Now trust me when I say this, you can't educate a person you don't love, respect or culturally understand. I truly believe there are a lot of young people in school who are not being loved, respected or culturally understood. For over 400 years we have been taught a European curriculum. With all the education we have received, we are still required to go to someone else to educate our children. So I ask the question, 'Are we educated or are we educated No-Grows?' I truly believe we are not educated we are indoctrinated. It takes 13 years to indoctrinate a person!!

Imagine for a moment that you live in a land where a number of the citizens have purple hair. Now suppose that most non-purple-haired people feel a little uneasy about the purple-haired fold; especially the males. And what if the vague prejudice extended even to little boys in school; who, because of the color of their hair, were apt to hear both these following messages, regularly: purple-haired boys aren't as smart as normal-haired boys; and, they need more discipline–after all, look at all the purple-haired criminals on television.
Suppose teachers went so far as to relegate some of these kids into separate classrooms so that they didn't interfere with the learning of others.
Now imagine that you have a purple-haired boy of your own–a terrific kid whose intelligence and potential, shines clearly. But after a few years in grade school, the light of his enthusiasm for

learning is beginning to dim. His teachers say it's his fault–that he can't do the work, won't stay on task, has a learning disability, rotten attitude, bad habits; you name it. What would you do?

As implausible as it sounds, this parable is all too real for some African American families with boys in the nation's public schools. Granted, not every black male student, in every learning environment, is suffering these biases; nor is it only the fault of the schools making.

The more fortunate students receive enough love, encouragement, and support at school, at home, or in their communities to achieve, in spite of the odds. But some black boys do not. Far too many confront a stifling kind of bias that destroys their interest in school, according to a growing chorus of educators and activists. This prejudice can have hurtful consequences: cultural insensitivity, lowered expectations, unduly harsh discipline, and the systematic shunting of African American boys into remedial or special education classes. Although the hardships some black male students face are not insurmountable, these problems must first be understood before they can be resolved. So that's why I say the Miss-Education of the No-Grow.

Notes

Rickie Clark

Quote

"The function of education is to teach one to think intensively and to think critically. Intelligence plus character - that is the goal of true education."

~Dr. Martin Luther King Jr.

CHAPTER 5
To Give Back or Go Back

When slavery officially ended in the United States, many black families began to migrate across the south, north, and west in search of opportunity, land and the ability to exercise new found freedoms without the threat of domestic terrorism. Having toiled the fields and factories of America for over 300 years without pay, black people emerged from slavery as the most skilled labor force in the country. As a result, black townships began to spring up and thrive in the late 1800s on into the early 1900s.

Where there were no townships, black people generally built their own communities and lived amongst themselves. These often were not exactly an oasis of freedom, however, these communities were being subjected to Jim Crow laws as well as economic, political, and terroristic control by whites.

This segregation system, while preventing and limiting Black mobility and political participation also perhaps inadvertently, turned our communities into business incubators, with our dollars circulating amongst black owned businesses several times before leaving the community. Entrepreneurs like Madame C.J. Walker, Marcus Garvey, Elijah Muhammad, and more were able to build business empires by providing quality products to African Americans that were not available to us in the general public.

While blacks that migrated to certain urban areas were forced to live in slums, many black communities and townships in other areas thrived economically in spite of the overt racism of the day. The typical black community during the Jim Crow era consisted of several businesses, churches, and schools primarily funded by the people who lived there. Black couples were the most married in America, and many of our elders love to speak of the time when the community was so safe that you could "leave your screen door open."

What happened? When did the African American community become something to "leave", rather than something to "develop"? Is the black community a place our ancestors chose to live, or a place that we were forced to live? When you look at the Asian community, Italian community, Irish community, and/or Jewish community, you see areas where these groups choose to concentrate their population in order to practice and preserve cultural norms, strengthen the ties between families, and organize to stay connected with people in their country of origin.

Of course plenty of people from these groups also live in other communities however, the cultural connection with the group they come from remain available, thriving, and intact. In many of these communities family businesses exist that have been open for generations. They maintain political and economic control of their own community and even have mechanisms in place to prevent the culture of their community from changing.

African Americans have spent a lot of time, energy, and money breaking down the cultural barriers set up in these communities in the name of "racial progress". But in doing so, have we chosen to neglect the development and growth of our own communities? Have we decided that there should be no "white communities" or "black communities", and in our dedication to this goal, have we left the African American community open for attack, gentrification, and economic/political disenfranchisement?

I think a community should reflect the collective culture of its inhabitants. The majority population in that community should also be the majority of land and business owners, political representatives, educators, and other leaderships. When a community is disenfranchised, the majority population doesn't control the economics and/or politics of that area. In many African American communities today, we're witnessing less than 1% business ownership, while making up more than 70-80% of the area's population. We elect African American candidates with our votes, yet their campaigns are often funded by institutions outside of the

African American community that don't have our best interest at heart.

Many of us who have "made it out", of the communities we grew up in, share fond memories, express love and dedication to that community, yet would never consider moving back or making a significant investment in its future. We are proud of the fact that we "give back", by visiting the local high school, attending our childhood church, and driving our cars in the occasional Black History Month parade. In the meantime your property taxes go toward enhancing the community you live in, the majority of your daily expenditures go to businesses in the community you live in, your children go to school in the community you live in, which continues to benefit and flourish while the one you grew up in, continues to deteriorate. It's no longer enough to just "give back", to our communities. If the African American community is going to survive, it's time for us to "go back", to our communities. A community should reflect the culture of its residents. We have a beautiful culture, a unique culture, as African Americans. We come from the oldest people on the planet earth. We've survived the worst crime against humanity in history. We've contributed to the landscape of America via music, art, science, industry, spirituality, linguistics, etc.; yet our children have little or no access to the fullness of our story in local schools.

I guarantee you can learn about Italy in Little Italy. I guarantee, you can learn about China in Chinatown. Does the African American community reflect the history and glory of Africa and/or the journey and immense contributions of African

Americans? One hundred fifty plus years "up from slavery", and we're still trying to *escape* where we live. Somewhere between the fall of Jim Crow and the rise of *integration*, we seemed to have decided that our community isn't worth saving. We've decided that to live there is a sign of failure. We've seemed to have bought into the racist notion that the crime and poverty in our community has less to do with systemic racism and a lack of opportunities, and more to do with the African American's inherent criminality. We call it the "hood," perhaps because everyone's goal is to no longer be a *neighbor*. To "give back" or to "go back". That is the question…

      Neighborhoods that are mainly African American and mainly low-income weren't just recently created.
African American communities across the yet to be United States; such as, Chicago, Detroit, Philadelphia, and Harlem were intentionally created by governments, landowners and policy makers. They wanted to systemically keep people of color out of white neighborhoods. Like so much of the numerous anti-African American policies that exist in the United States today, the creation of African American neighborhoods began with slavery. Even though all Northern states had passed legislation that abolished slavery by 1804, abolishment was not complete and immediate throughout the North. For example, Pennsylvania passed the Act for the Gradual Abolition of Slavery in 1780; yet by 1850, hundreds of African Americans were still enslaved. Even with the complete abolition of slavery, African Americans were not given the full benefits of citizenship or personhood in Northern states. Many

Northern white abolitionists didn't advocate for full integration or equity for African American people. The legacy of slavery continued through segregationist and discriminatory laws that were seethed in anti-Blackness. Even European immigrants, such as the Irish or Italian actively benefited from anti-African American racism. Hence, the whole idea of Jim Crow and segregation of the races really originated in the North. This isn't to say that 'African American-only' neighborhoods have only grown out of segregationist laws many were actively created as safe spaces where communities could thrive and succeed.

However, it's important to understand the history of how African American neighborhoods had to be created, because of systemic violence, segregationist laws, and discriminatory practices. Additionally, the creations of these neighborhoods weren't limited to the South. Northern anti-Blackness was just as prominent, if not more covert. These attitudes and policies also have continued well into the 21st century. Starting in the 1900s, the following policies are just a few ways that African American neighborhoods have been created and systemically marginalized.

1) Post-Reconstruction, white supremacy was visibly rampant across the South;
2) African Americans experienced widespread violence;
3) Public lynching's to wide-scaled massacres.

Meanwhile, the North was experiencing an economic boom. Especially during World War I, there was a massive need for cheap industrial labor. These are two critical reasons for the Great

Migration, a massive movement of Black people migrating from the South to the North. The African American populations of West & East Coast and mid-western cities like Los Angeles, Chicago, Boston, and Cleveland increased by a hundredfold. White lawmakers and landowners began creating discriminatory policies. For example, they ensured that African Americans, even wealthy ones, couldn't move into white neighborhoods. Second, they ensured that African American neighborhoods wouldn't receive economic-growth funding of any kind from the government keeping them impoverished. Essentially restrictive covenants are agreements amongst folks in a neighborhood binding them to not sell, lease, or rent to people, based on their race. Restrictive covenants were used across cities in the North during the early 1900s in order to stop African Americans from moving into white neighborhoods. Formal deeds were drawn-up in order to stop property owners from renting and selling to African Americans.

And here we are in 2019 with even more startling statistics: 1) In America, in Asia communities a dollar circulates among the community's banks, retailers and business professionals for up to 28 days before it is spent with outsiders. In the Jewish community, the circulation period is 19 days. Hispanics keep their dollar for 7 days. But in the Black community, the dollar lives six hours!

2) Over 60% of the Fortune 500's minority spend - the contracts, the products on the shelves, the suppliers they use - with Asian owned businesses used to be spent with Black owned businesses. That's why

when you go to your grocery store, whole aisles for Hispanic and Asian food products, made by Hispanic and Asian companies.

3) Lillian Bettencourt, owner L'Oreal, largest Black brands in the world #12 on the Forbes list with $12.7 billion in assets. Lillian is the proud owner of L'Oreal (Lancome, SofSheen Carson, Kiehls, Shu Uemura and Armani).

4) Sixty - eighty percent of Hennessy's global revenues come from African Americans.

5) This is a good read. Ever hear of an all-Black town, in Greenwood, Oklahoma? The town flourished with home ownership all Black businesses of banks, hotels, grocery stores, movie houses and schools. In 1921 the small town was attacked by White men acting as police. The town was burned to the ground. Thousands were left homeless and hundreds lost their lives.

Http://www.ebony.com/black-history/destruction-of-black-wall-street/

6) "... Never stop and forget that collectively, that means all of us together, collectively we are richer than all the nations in the world.

We have an annual income of more than thirty billion dollars a year, which is more than all of the exports of the United States, and more than the national budget of Canada. Did you know that? That's power right there, if we know how to pool it."- Martin Luther King Jr. Come back or go back?

Notes

Quote

Africans must know their own history for it is needed to correctly read the language of their own MIND, language that is still expressing unconscious ideas in Ancient African Tongue. African History is essential for African Mental Health and the transformation of African Mental Slaves into AFRICAN MASTERS.

~Dr. Richard King, M.D.

Rickie Clark

Chapter 6
N's Are Only Made in America

    I know that the title is hard to hear but the reality is even worse. Only in America are we called Niggers. That's why I say Niggers are made in America. The word nigger itself is a noun, Webster defines Nigger as:

    used as an insulting and contemptuous for a member of any dark-skinned race.

    a member of a class or group of people who are systematically subjected to discrimination and unfair treatment Origin: alteration of earlier neger, from Middle French negre, from Spanish or Portuguese negro, from negro black, from Latin niger. First use: 1574

So be it in 1574 what human puts a label on another human?

In Anthony T. Browder's book, *From The Browder File,* he states, in most European languages, the word for black was typically associated with aspects of death. The word death is derived from the Greek necro, which means dead, and is similar in sound and meaning to the word negro. Throughout European history the words necro and negro were commonly used to reference the physical, spiritual or mental death of a person, place or thing.

So this is why I say Niggers are made in America. To my knowledge I don't know of any other race of people or category of humans who take a negative connotation and embrace it as their own.

Similar to a quote from Dr. Frances Cress Welsing: "We wonder why we're not making progress . . . We're the only people on this entire planet who have been taught to sing and praise our demeanment. I'm a bitch. I'm a hoe. I'm a thug. I'm a dog. If you can train people to demean and degrade themselves, you can oppress them forever. You can even program them to kill themselves and they won't even understand what happened."

That's why I say Niggers are made in America. By now you're probably asking who are making the Niggers and how are they making the Niggers? Glad you asked. So let me put it this way. Do you know how a baby zebra knows who his mother and father are when they come out of the females womb? So let me help you, when the baby zebras are dropped from the mother, both parents circle the baby zebra continuously until the baby zebra memorizes the stripes of their parents. Once the baby zebra memorizes the stripes he or she knows who to follow. What kinds of stripes do our children see between kindergarten and 12th grade? They see lack of education or no education at all, disrespect and distrust of our women our culture and everything that is African.

In the yet to be United States of America when slavery was in play, when enslaved Africans were brought from Africa as soon as they got off the boat the mother and father was taken to a far away plantation and the children would be raised by other people. In other words, *white* people were telling them who they are and showing them that they have no history.

I get upset when anyone uses the "N" word, but more so when people of other races use it, here's why. That word has been used to oppress and offend for so many years and it's wrong to hear it come out of anyone's mouth. It is overly offensive when I hear other races (we may as well say white people) use it, because their ancestors are the originators of the hatred so I can't help but be on guard. We say that times have changed, which they have, but we still need to realize that racism is alive and prevalent. That word was created for hate and I get so tired of people trying to act as if what black people went through in this country is a thing of the past. Slavery is still an issue. And if and when it is ever not an issue you can bet I'll be dead long before. And the slow process is not because we don't want to not be an issue (though I'm sure there are some that wouldn't mind). It's because it was such a powerful blow and horrible way to start. We did not come willingly as so many other immigrants did. We were forced, beaten and told we were less than dogs. So no, please don't act as if we are not justified in our feelings because I promise, you will never have to deal with it like I have. You may sympathize, you may think racism is really bad, but there is nothing to compare to walking down the street with brown skin on your back. More importantly, I'm absolutely disgusted by African-Americans that use that word against each other and then get hypocritical when another race does. They make it okay by even saying it. It's not okay though, I hate that word. African-Americans are split in half. One half is the ignorant do-nothing, gripe to the government side, and the other is the driven, smart, resourceful, and goal-oriented, average, respectable African-American. The do-nothings make the other half look just as stupid as them but they're far from it. They work hard (sometimes twice as hard) as everyone else does to move up in society and get a good education. The upwardly-mobile African-Americans have a problem with the other half of the blacks because other races(Asians, Europeans, and other races) don't know the difference between one black and another. Then everything that the truly respectable ones are trying to achieve for their race, the ignorant ones are undoing. Therefore, you can see how it's not okay for every black person to say it, most conscious ones would never. Any black who know of Dr. Martin Luther King Jr., or Rosa Parks would acknowledge and appreciate everything they fought for just so future blacks could have a fighting chance and those blacks would never try and desensitize a word that is so utterly hateful and disgusting. For us to say that word, they are, in a way, enslaving themselves and tying themselves to a word that should have long been out of the language. However, like I said, us African-Americans are truly divided and the gap only grows wider every time that word is used as a term of "endearment" to our kind.

Throughout the history of slavery we were called that by white people as a way of looking down on us like we were insignificant. Nowadays the African American youth are the only ones you will hear calling each other that word because they know they are not offending each other. For another race to call them the 'n' word would be highly offensive because people already know it is. Therefore they feel the person who is calling them that thinks they are better than they are. In short, don't say that word. People of that race have worked long and hard to get where they are today and deserve to be treated with respect and dignity.

Kindergarten to 12th Grade Can = 13 Years A Slave

Notes

Rickie Clark

Quote

"A people without the knowledge of their past history, origin, or
culture, is like a tree without roots.
If you have no confidence in self,
you are twice defeated in the race of life."
~Marcus Garvey

Chapter 7
Racial Equity Walk

I was first introduced to the Racial Equity Walk while participating in a courageous conversation about race in 2016. Glenn Singleton, author of the *"Courageous Conversations About Race,"* talks about a racial equity walk. I have participated in a few trainings: Beyond Diversity, Courageous Conversation; and, How to Talk to Youth About Race to name a few. After gathering information from these trainings, I began to contemplate on the fact that we the adults, are receiving the training and we're explaining how race affects us on how we stand. But the youth haven't had the opportunity to experience the training themselves. I began to think if this training affected me how would it affect the youth. To illustrate, we're all sitting under the same electrical lighting but it's effecting us differently. Because I can tell you how the light is affecting me from where I'm standing; you can tell how it's affecting you from where you're standing. So until we get the perspective of our youth we're going in the wrong direction. We must first explain to them Racial Equity is both and effect and a procedure. Now, why do I say that, you ask. I can't solve your problems from where I stand and you can't solve their problems from where you stand. Our problems are where we are and their problems are from where they are.

    I went back to the school district and began to walk the halls of the schools where I mentor. As the director, I am responsible for the designing, implementation and coordinating programs to help young men of color transition from one life stage to another. This is the initiative funded by the department of Racial Equity and Excellence at the Fort Worth Independent School District. The MBK program is implemented in the elementary, middle and high schools. Meetings are held at the schools and most times we would meet in different classrooms, the auditorium and even the library. We meet with participants on a weekly basis, once a week during their lunch and we always provide food to substitute their cafeteria lunch. We call it, Lunch and Learn, it is where we provide liberating information.

    In our Racial Equity walk, I would ask the young men to line-up from the shortest to the tallest. I would let them know that this shows evolution, from boys to men. I would also explain to them that this is a non-verbal exercise. I inform them that people will be watching and wondering why they're showing such discipline and I remind them not to talk.

The young men are told to point to things in the library that shows their culture in a positive light. Then the participants were asked to go on a scavenger hunt to find books that speak positive of people of color. As always they would find no more than two posters on the walls and not much more on the shelves. Sometimes just three to four books could be found that spoke positive of their culture. So for every picture, poster, artifact and book that the youths would find, I would take a picture of the items and where they were located. Students after the activity were asked to get in touch with their feelings. I remind them that this is a nonverbal exercise.

At this point the students are really ready to talk but because we want them to get in-touch with their feelings we encourage them to remain quiet. They are asked to return to the classroom, pick up their food, go to their seats and to not speak at this point until they have completed their meal. After eating the dialog starts. They were asked, "How did it make you feel not seeing things on the shelves that spoke positively about you or your culture?"

This is where it gets ugly. Here are the responses:

"It made me mad, before this activity, I never noticed it till now. It made me feel like they don't care about me or my people."

"I wish I was white."

"Mr. Rickie, I read all the time and I come to the library all the time but until today, I never even noticed; I feel sick."

I often wonder, why don't we know our history.

A question from students that I'm often asked, "Why don't they want us to know our history?"

One student even said to me, "Mr. Clark do you think we can really make a change?" My response, "I can't, but you can."

A quote According to Emily Penner and Thomas Dee "... *Ethnic Studies participation increased student attendance (i.e., reduce unexcused absences) by 21 percentages points, cumulative ninth-grade GPA by 1.4 grade points, and credits earned by 23 credits. These GPA gains were larger for boys than for girls as well as higher in math and science than in ELA. Overall, our findings indicate that a culturally relevant curriculum implemented in a strongly supportive context can be highly effective at improving outcomes among a diverse group of academically at-risk student."* (2016; 3).

Despite the miss information given about people of color, taught in public, charter and private schools, as well as reinforced on television, movies, etc.; I believe that if true history was taught to us as part of the school curriculum, it would reveal how the world has been lying to us. I say this because, how do you explain 400 years of hiding the truth about a people's history and culture so I encourage you to do a Racial Equity walk in your public library, your museums and your schools.

Don't forget to do an important Racial Equity Walk through your home. As you walk from room to room ask yourself, 'What in this room shows that I am African?'

Kindergarten to 12th Grade Can = 13 Years A Slave

Notes

Rickie Clark

RACIAL BIOGRAPHIES

Kindergarten to 12th Grade Can = 13 Years A Slave

Eagle in a Chicken Coop
Pharoah Davis

I was born an Eagle but told I was a chicken

They told me my wings are ugly

My feet too big

And how I look different from the other chicken kids

I've been teased, taunted and talked about the same

Started believing Ugly, Stupid, and Poor was my name

I've always felt out of place, and never knew why

Always had dreams of soaring the sky

With these big ugly wings you would think I could fly

But they keep telling me don't even try... to jump nor fly

Just dream... within the box they've created for my life

I've been given a chicken education with no history of my kind

None of the founding fathers have features like mine

And when we pay homage to their predecessors...

I often think about my ancestors

Those from whom I come

Who fly high in the noon sky, circling the sun

Zooming past the moon

Rickie Clark

With a wealth of wisdom others can't consume

My ancestors speak, telling me to listen with my intuition

Follow my heart and press towards my mission

No matter what others say, I am mighty and strong

In the school of chickens is Not where I belong

So...I will study my own history in search of my truth

I will always question, and explore to find my R.o.o.t.s

Restoration of our true story

Talk with elders to discover our glory

of ancient days when we soared the skies

over Pyramids by the Pharaohs

and mount Kilimanjaro 40 miles high

My story isn't just a mystery

And my beauty reflects my identity

I am an Eagle with strength and pride

I will spread my wings and glide

Kindergarten to 12th Grade Can = 13 Years A Slave

over your chicken feed lies

That have kept me bound and scared to leave the ground

But now I see who I am meant to be

Master of flight, descendant of kings

Ruler of Sky, over land and sea

The mighty majestic Eagle...is Me

Rickie Clark

Essay
~Tony D. Hudson

As a small child I learned that race mattered. My father believed the only way to succeed in America was through education. Big Tony, as our family called my father, shouted through his wide toothy Magic Johnson like smile and gold lined left tooth, "Dr. T," whenever I would enter a room. My father also believed that the only way for me to survive in a world so cold for so many of the Black folks he knew was to figure out what White people have and do, and to get this for myself. Big Tony wanted Little Tony, as my family referred to me, to leave conversations about race and racism alone, and be like White people. To this day my father and I talk often about what I see as a society still hobbled by a shredded achilles called racism. Big Tony still sees a society that only allows a Black person to survive so long as they don't significantly upset White people. As a champion for racial equity you might imagine I have had to do a lot of centering work to get ready for conversations about race with my father.

My mother approached race in a completely different way, yet with the same hopes and dreams of her children surviving in a White dominated world. Rose, as other people call my mother, will tell anyone the same story if the topic is about getting my siblings and I through Pre-K-12 education:

"I had to stay on him or Tony would only do what he had to to get by in school; school came easy to him. Ask Tony and he will tell you, he spent many days staring out that screen door on punishment for playing around in school. I had to stay on him, but I also had to stay on them White teachers every year; like clock-work one of his teachers would be willing to help him fail, or act like he couldn't do the work. He's been a school Principal, a Director of Equity, and now he coaches Superintendents and Principals across the country because I stayed on him and the schools, they don't believe Black children can learn the same as White children right off the bat. Any parent of a Black child that isn't up at that school holding them accountable, and looking at what's going on between their child and the teacher is giving the school a license to fail their child. You better be up there checking on those teachers, talking to the Principal, making friends with board members, and joining the local NAACP to make sure they treat your child right as a Black child. This is just how it goes when you Black. What Tony needs to do in his consulting job is just tell all the Black parents that, and if they listen then their kids will be successful."

My mother ensured from a young age that innocence, or ignorance, around race was never a value that my sister, little brother, or I internalized. Rose, as other folks called her, made it clear that having Black skin in Pre-K-12 education would be a daily battle for human dignity in systems that have learned to love Black children the least.

Rickie Clark

When I was in high school my mother organized the Association of Black Lawyers, the Chief of Police, the Mayor, and a group of Black parents in our small segregated city of Omaha, Nebraska, birthplace of Malcolm X, to demand a public apology for an egregious coordinated racist attack on me and my friends. The police department, downtown businesses, and popular local news stations staged a televised surprise mass arrest of all the Black children walking downtown to the bus from Omaha Central High School. The charge levied against us was that someone in the past caused a problem with a motorist, and we were all jaywalking. Yes, we were butted up against the concrete sides of the massive block long building with horses until each shade of our Black wrists were locked with tight plastic handcuffs. We were not all placed in the patty wagons until the second wave, the civilian element of the surprise brigade, were perfectly positioned to get our angry and screaming Black faces square into the view of the large bulky news cameras and invasive microphones. It was in our DNA to try to conjure protest songs as we were shoved into the patty wagons, this was in our DNA.

We were lower income growing up, so we only knew lawyers when someone got into trouble or were about to get paid after being hit by a bus, or slipping on wet grocery store tiles. More than 25 years later, I am still in awe of my 5 foot nothing, one of 14 sibling, high school diploma, smoked meat queen, racial equity champion of a mother organizing all those people to ensure the lives of her Black son and his friends mattered. This would not be the first time, as she would later organize the NAACP to finally integrate the White dance squad at my alma matter; they loved taking my sisters' music mixes and dance moves, yet consistently told her and the other Black girls they didn't have the dance training for dance team in a school that was likely half Black, or more.

While I love my father, it is my mother who was my first racial equity champion. Through her courage, organic community organizing, and persistent fight for racial justice in the education of her children is how I developed a racial equity purpose of my own.

I would go on to experience countless examples of my mother's theory in action in grade school, college, as a Principal, and as a school district Director of Equity. My most painful confirmation of Rose's theory occurred when I led my school as the Principal well beyond the 90th percentile in the state of Minnesota for the rate at which we were eliminating racial disparities. Regardless of our "achieve gap" closing success, only some celebrated, and many saw excellence in learning from Black and Brown children under the leadership of a Black male as a threat more than proof of the possibilities in Pre-K-12 education systems. In hindsight it is not the racial equity academic achievement of the children that stuck with me the most, but the work of so many community leaders, educators, youth, and organizers for racial justice that partnered with me as the Director of Equity later to gain a commitment from the school board and district to expand racial equity as a focus to every school and department in the school system. The courage instilled in me by my mother, and my practice to Stay Engaged in Courageous Conversations About Race (Singleton, 2015) with my father, no matter how upset his views made me, nurtured the will, skill, and passion I needed to courageously engage in transformational partnerships with brave educators and community leaders to spread racial equity transformation to a whole school system.

My purpose on earth is to organize racial consciousness. That means that I am looking to build powerful relationships with an inter-racial and intra-racial coalition of people and resources aligned to the common interest of taking a more courteous and powerful approach to achieving systemic structural racial equity. While I do not believe I will complete this purpose before I die, it is essential that in my old age my children, grand, and great great grand children hear from an endless number of people who tell their stories of how I partnered with them to unapologetically transform their lives and communities toward greater racial equity i the world.

It is because of my purpose as a racial equity leader that I surround myself with people committed to racial justice and healing in education and beyond. I surround myself with racial equity heroes in education like Glenn Singleton and my Courageous Conversation family. I follow courageous racial justice faith organizers like Pastor Paul Slack of New Creation Church of Minneapolis, Minnesota. My purpose is why I have spent time on every trip to Fort Worth at The Doc Bookshop where I learn from the powerful sisters that run the only Black owned book shop and community gathering space in the Fort Worth Dallas Metroplex (Special shout out to the amazing family at Doc Bookshop as I coincidentally found out that they hail from my birth town of Omaha, Nebraska!). While school systems across this nation struggle with Black children the most, The Doc Bookshop, like world heavy weight champion Terrence "Bud" Crawford out of Omaha, have the winning combination for eliminating racism in Pre-K-12 education and beyond right on their bookshelves. I implore everyone to stop by The Doc Bookshop and pick out a book from several racial equity in education heroes that have changed my life like Anthony Browder, Beverly Daniels Tatum, Gloria Ladson-Billings, Derick Bell and so many others that have the keys to achieving equity in Pre-K-12 education and beyond. My purpose is why I have learned so much from watching the most courageous Brown brother board member that I know, Jacinto Ramos. My purpose, inspired early on by the spirit of racial justice that my mother carried, is what led me say yes to writing this essay at the request of another one of my racial equity justice heroes, brother Rickie Clark.

My dear brother Rickie, I am learning from you all the time, and so will my children. I am in awe at how you courageously and gently hold the spirits and development of so many Black and Brown brothers and sisters of all ages in the city of Fort Worth and beyond.

Rickie Clark

Every time I am in Fort Worth you provide me a front row seat to the respect and transformational relationships you have crafted in the schools, and in the larger community, with your powerful leadership of My Brother's Keeper, and with the awesome community gathering and learning space at The Doc Bookshop. In the spirit of being "studied" as an African, as you often say, you are an exemplar of the Kemetic guidance that implores us to Know Thyself, Be Obsessed with Distinguishing Knowledge from Foolishness, and to Build for Eternity. My Brother, you are Building for Eternity and I am glad to be doing so with you.

Toward equity, together.

Tony D. Hudson

Tony is a leader for racial equity, and beneficiary of the racial justice seeking community. Tony is also an Equity Transformation Specialist with Courageous Conversation (CourageousConversation.com) where he works with leaders across the United States to engage systemic racial equity transformation.

Kindergarten to 12th Grade Can = 13 Years A Slave

Essay
~Minister Lee Muhammad
Of Muhammad Mosque#52
Forth Worth, TX

My earliest memory of the education I received took place in Dallas, Texas in a community referred to as Pleasant Grove. The neighborhood in which I resided and the school I attended were both predominantly white.

On the grade school level, I remember absolutely nothing about any black history being taught. Me and my other 4 black classmates sensed the difference in the attention and treatment of our white classmates and were instinctively aware of the reality of race. The white students differed in the pride that they had in themselves which reflected in their demeanor.

Whatever education I received in black culture came through television on Saturday mornings, when I would watch Fat Albert and the Gang, which I did religiously. I loved the show within the show, "The Brown Hornet ". Unfortunately, it was not the Brown Hornet that I really admired most, because my mind was saturated with the white super heroes who were the only ones to be taken seriously.

Due to a divorce between my parents, I moved to another part of the city referred to as Oak Cliff. This is when I experienced what is commonly called a "cultural shock". The schools I would attend now would be predominantly black. Was there a difference? Yes, I was receiving the same "education" but the sense of self pride was not there. I went from seeing no fights to several throughout the year. Again, the "education" was relatively the same. We studied general history of great rulers and leaders both modern and ancient. There was Alexander the Great, Caesar, and Napoleon. American History consisted of the Founding Fathers, the Civil War, Pearl Harbor and of course we can never forget The Alamo.

Moving toward my senior year something different happened, it was the phenomenon of what would come to be called conscious rap. It was through the likes of KRS 1 and Public Enemy that I began to learn about my history and the outstanding heroes and leaders that stood up and spoke for me. It was through these rap songs, that for the first time I would hear the names of Malcolm X, The Honorable Elijah Muhammad and The Honorable Minister Louis Farrakhan. The interesting thing about Public Enemy was that on the cover of the vinyl album, they had the words to every recording. I will never forget the day I pulled it out, played the album while simultaneously reading every word they rapped. The last song was "Party For Your Right To Fight". The last words to that song would change the trajectory of my life. Chuck D rapped, "Words from the Honorable Elijah Muhammad, know who you are to be black". This raised two questions. 1) Who was Elijah Muhammad and all these other black leaders and why haven't I heard of them? 2) Who am I to be black? I went to the school library and checked out The Autobiography of Malcolm X. This set me on a journey to read all the books I could, pertaining to the marvelous history of our ancestors. Now I knew what was missing in my earlier education. It was a sense of purpose. Now I felt that pride in myself and it began to show in my demeanor and behavior.

My initial feeling at the start of my journey was anger. Angry because I had went through twelve years of school not being taught this rich history that in truth was the history of America and the history of the world. However that anger was directed into concentrated self study. Because I felt a need to make up for "lost time", I spent a lot of time in the public and school library as well as black owned book stores.

I honestly wished that I could have traveled back in time. If my parents had this knowledge and taught me not just to read but to read material that gave me a sense of reason, purpose and self knowledge, perhaps I would have displayed that same confidence that my white counterparts displayed when they eagerly raised their hand to answer questions raised by the teacher. Perhaps I would not have sat there wondering what good is all this information and how can I apply it in my life. Maybe I would not have felt offended when I did put forth an effort and my own people would accuse me of "trying to act white". I could have easily responded, " If reading and being smart is acting white, then what is acting black? Then I could have proceeded to teach them about Timbuktu, that great African center of learning where books and learning were a way of life.

In hindsight I can see that 1989 was a turning point among black youth at that time. We were all brought to a crossroad. Due to the rise in consciousness that was spreading through movies and music, many of my classmates began to wear African medallions and t-shirts reflecting this new found pride. In the world of media there was the thesis and antithesis. In the movie industry there was Spike Lees' Do The Right Thing and then there was Colors and Boys In Da Hood. On the other end of what would come to be called conscious rap music was another genre that would come to be labeled gangster rap. Unfortunate as it was, I saw many that I grew up with and would graduate with become involved in criminal activities and eventually spend time in jail. When asked, what influenced their decisions? They said that it was the gangster rap. These were the choices we were confronted with. A proper education allows us to properly interpret the information and messages we receive. In my opinion, this shows the power of positive messages and the proper study of history. When I found out what was, then I knew how to respond to what is. The more I studied the history of the great men and women of my people and what they struggled for and accomplished. A rich legacy was left behind and I felt duty bound to pick up the torch.

The missing ingredient in my education was the question, Who am I? Once I got that question answered it would influence every decision that I would make up to this point in my life. The friends I would choose, the places I would go or stay away from. The decision to get married and stay married for now 26 years. Taking care of myself and my family and of course my service to the wider community.

It has been said that one's attitude determines ones altitude. The more I knew self, I would love self and take on the attitude of mastery. This taught me that the knowledge of self is the key to all learning. Only when we know our history in the world, can we take up where our forebears left off and work to get us back to where we belong.

Rickie Clark

Essay
~Amon Rashidi

If you take me from my homeland against my will, that's not slavery, that's kidnapping. If you castrate me to instill fear and cut my foot off when I run, that's not slavery, that's terrorism. If you force yourself on women and children for your sexual pleasure, that's not slavery, that's rape. If you strip me of my name, language, religion, culture, values, norms, and my family; that's not slavery, that's genocide. What was waged against my people was a war redefined as slavery. These are crimes against humanity. Whoever controls the mind of your children, controls the destiny of your race. So a man thinketh so he is.

Who do our children think they are and who told them? Before you answer remember you were that kid yesterday, being indoctrinated and redefined by stereotypes, myths, and historical lies. Having to sue the very school system that you seek to educate you and your children (Brown vs Board of Education), to be treated fair and equal.

So at its origin, our history with the educational system is problematic at best. Ask yourself the question, how many books, stories, positive images, did you see hear and learn about Black people as you completed your high school education? Now compare that to the countless material we were mandated to learn about whites from kindergarten to high school. Whoever controls the narrative, controls the story, so while attending the first phase of organized education (preschool and kindergarten) you don't see the most important thing necessary for your future; you.

Using the Rashidi Stage metric, let's examine this as you age through the educational process. The first stage is age 0 - 8, defined as Internalization. This is your life's first introduction to the world. Observation, the act, and process of observing something to gain information for human development. This is crucial to our children, especially now, considering the current climate where people of color are treated more like suspects as opposed to citizens. Remember, our children are internalizing this behavior and images shape our children's reality. What they see reflects what they feel, what they feel reflects what they think, how they think reflects how they act and how they act dictates how others will react to them. This is the most impressionable and impacted stage of our children's lives and they learn, little to nothing, about themselves or their people. This process makes you question the importance of your contribution to the world you are being taught to enter. Not only do you see this absence, so does the world, leaving them and others to question your role and importance.

The second stage is ages 9-13, defined as Experimentation. You now move into this state with artificial norms, based off the lies, stereotypes, and myths you observed and have accepted through stage one, Internalization. Combine this with puberty and peer pressure, then you do the math. You begin to experiment with terminology like, "What's up my nigga?". If it's popular, accepted and peer approved, it's now your new artificial reality. It becomes clear now that you don't know who you are so you began to play a role, but now you don't know how to come out of character.

You now take this experimental phase into stage three, ages 14-19, defined as Socialization. You now begin to socialize your thoughts, feelings, emotions and actions. Socializing a reality not your own, a history not your own; most importantly, an identity, not your own. Spreading misgivings, myths and lies based on a false representation of your self. This is now reinforced through organized education, popular culture, mass media, internalized belief, and practice. Many times during this stage we feel disconnected and incomplete. This is from a lack of true self identity because the right knowledge will correct the wrong behavior. But if you begin with a lie, you end with a lie; especially if you don't know the truth. This makes your history a matter of discovery as oppose to development and your purpose a matter of popularity as oppose to passion.

The last and final stage is age 20 and beyond, defined as Realization. A summation of all the realities you've endured and have accepted from stage one through stage three.
>	A final analysis of your current mentality that,
>	if not interrupted or adjusted
>	could equal twelve years a slave?

Color Conscious
By Jacinto Ramos

My first encounter with race was when I was in third grade in a pubic school. I recall being on the playground with two classmates. They had been picking on me throughout the day so I decided to defend myself when we got to recess. It was a big mistake. The twins put a beat down on me (or so I thought). For years my recollection of the fight was something that would have been seen in a Bruce Lee film. It included jumping kicks and round house kicks.
The truth is, they simply pushed me down and I sobbed all the way back to the classroom.

When I got home, I told my parents what happened. My father asked me what color they were. That is my first memory of my first encounter with race. The twins were Black. Society had begun to teach me that Black people were lazy, aggressive and not very intelligent.

The following year I began to attend a Catholic school located in the heart of my neighborhood. There was maybe one or two students that did not racially identify as LatinX/Brown. The remainder of my elementary and middle school years were alongside predominantly Brown students. My teachers however, were primarily White. The police officers in my community were predominantly White. The business owners were predominantly White. From third grade and on, I began to notice color in my life.

Rickie Clark

In high school I became hypersensitive as race seemed to completely surround me. I received a partial scholarship to play sports at the only Catholic high school in the county. The campus was not racially diverse and there were only a handful of Brown students. I was reminded on a daily basis that I was different and not always welcome. On the football field and basketball court, I was referenced as "The Wetback" from time to time. Although I am certain my classmates didn't always mean it to be so hurtful…it cut deep nonetheless.

I recall a breaking point was when I took some cousins and friends from my neighborhood to a party. Four of us were Brown and one was Black. My teammates met me at the door as they watched us walking up. They stated, "the party is over, just go home." The fact was that the party was not over. The music was loud and we could see a full house through the living room windows. I could see the look on the faces of my teammates and classmates. They were horrified at the idea of five guys from the hood coming into their house party.

When I got to college, I wanted to make sense of all the White Eurocentric academic material I was taught in private school. I could care less about Shakespeare or Mark Twain. I knew deep down inside there had to be more to an education. I yearned for academic material that spoke about my truth. Dr. Jose Angel Gutierrez fulfilled that need. He is one of the founders of La Raza Unida political party and he was my professor for two courses at the University of Texas at Arlington. He taught me different perspectives about the Texas Rangers, Kings Ranch, the Bracero Program, and countless of other moments that painted the Brown community in a negative light. The counter narratives sent me on a pilgrimage to find myself and my people. Trips to Acuna, Coahuila and Morelia, Michoacan allowed understanding of my family and ancestors. The experiences were refreshing because I began to learn my history from a point of liberation. I learned my indigenous people were never conquered by the Mexicas, otherwise known as the Aztecs. We didn't have to fight them…we simply negotiated with them. Each story about the intellectual capacity of my indigenous people filled my heart with pride. It was validating to learn my people were not destined to be drug dealers, gang bangers, alcoholics and/or abusers.

Crossing the border would always do something to my spirit. I could see myself in every child selling "chicles" and shining shoes on the plaza. The experiences gave me a privilege and became a reality in my life whenever I crossed the border. I asked myself, "Why me?" Why was I able to cross over and take advantage of all the benefits this country had to offer and why were there so many Brown people like me in Mexico dropping out of school to enter the workforce to provide for the home. Why were so many of my Brown brothers and sisters not completing school in America? What was it that I had and what was it that they needed.

Rickie Clark

As an adult I continue to wrestle with the social construct of race. I am of Mexican descent and proud of my Purepecha indigenous bloodline. I am confident in who I am and I believe I am connected to my ancestors. I can feel their love and pride as they watch me navigate and often circumnavigate White America. I am cognizant I was born and raised on indigenous land we now call America. Part of my journey is calling my brothers and sisters to consciousness and helping them become aware of how Whiteness shows up in their lives.

Sometimes it is enough by simply pronouncing my name correctly. Jacinto Ramos, Jr.

My parents were born in Mexico and did not have the privilege to complete their education. There was no way my father could have known his question would prompt me to become color conscious.

His journey to America was solely focused on giving me the opportunities he could not imagine. My three sons have experienced race in their own way. The difference is, our home is equipped with an education that can counter its negative intentions.

Race is working exactly the way it was designed to work. It continues to sustain disparities as well as a divided nation. In the Fort Worth Independent School District, we are countering by writing our own curriculum for people of color. American education systems do not teach students beyond the Black and White binary. It is evident when students cannot name 5 Brown and 5 Asian-American heroes/sheroes. We will ensure students coming out of Fort Worth ISD will be racially conscious and participate in their own liberation. They will be too woke to be broke (on knowledge).

Jacinto A. Ramos, Jr., is a statewide and national educational leader that specializes in educational policy, racial equity and board governance. He is a juvenile probation officer, school board president in Fort Worth Independent School District and an adjunct professor at Texas Christian University in Comparative Race & Ethnic Studies (CRES) department. He has been married to Anita Ramos for over 20 years and lives in the North Side of Fort Worth with his three sons; Marky, Danny and Sammy.

Rickie Clark

Unequal Education
Pharoah Davis

The purpose of the American education system

Is for students to learn about the world around them

To develop the ability to think and process information

Transfer knowledge that will be useful in contributing to this nation

That should be the standard for all children of America

But the Black and brown child are held to a different criteria

This school system is a system made for us... not by us.

Made for our position of servitude to a system we trust

One nation... under God... Invisible... no liberty

No justice for us.

But we still must... use those obstacles as stepping stones

We must take the second hand books and hand me down supplies

And still provide... a sufficient culture

of learning while yearning to be included.

This is how we did... when we taught our own kids

In that hour... when we had the power to educate our own

Kindergarten to 12th Grade Can = 13 Years A Slave

In our schools, in our homes

But when taught by them...

We still be, what we've always been... Unequal

Black boys are often treated as problems before treated as people

Exposed to extreme measures of subjugation

Labeled and placed in classes like Special education

First ones to be chastised, detained, or suspended

Last to be rewarded, uplifted, or commended

Last to be praised, first to be tased

or dazed by a curriculum that doesn't encouraged

our individuality, nor our creativity

The reality is this is the same system of Brown vs. Board of Education

50 years later, Black & Brown still bored with their Education

No inspiration, no real motivation to be creative and proud

Embracing our culture has not been allowed

13 years a Slave can very well describe

The experience of the education system over Black & Brown lives

We still invest in this system by sending our babies to that prison

Called the educational facility

A prerequisite for the correctional facility

No coincidence why we stand in line and raise our hand to speak

Work all day with a small break time to eat

When we don't follow suit we're put in detention

Depending on the act we may face suspension

Which is isolation... resulting in probation

Until graduation

I'm just stating the facts of a delicate situation

That must be addressed

When we taught our own we were at our best

Issues like low reading levels and ADD

which stands for African Diaspora Dilemma if you ask me

should be dealt with from a family perspective

Creatively connecting culturally should be the objective

The answers are not in simply regurgitating

Information by standardize test taking

Their standardize lies will only condone the demise of our children

Instead of professional test takers

We should be grooming future movers and shakers

And innovators

We are the teachers and builders of the world

Every Black & Brown boy and girl

Deserves exposure to the truth

It is our duty to get back to our R.O.O.T.S

Restoration Of Our True Selves

Our true stories, sharing the glory of who we really are

Our children are the recycled Stars

of our darkest nights...

the hopes and dreams of our tomorrow

the beacons of light in the midst of our sorrow

We cannot hand over their pure hearts and young minds,

to a system that's never cared about our kind,

And expect them to shine

We must rewind the clock and go back to a time

When we were taught by us... for us

Rickie Clark

which created leaders among us

who come back and continue to build us

as a community and a people...

That's the how we make education Equal.

APPENDIX A
50 African History Questions We all Should Know

1. What's the original name of Africa?
2. What is the name of the only continent that doesn't float on water?
3. Is Africa a country or continent?
4. How many countries are inside of Africa?
5. How much bigger is Africa than the United States?
6. Where is the birthplace of humanity and civilization?
7. Where were the oldest human bones found and were they male for female?
8. Name three natural resources found in Africa.
9. Name five countries in Africa.
10. What is the name of the longest river in the world?
11. What is the name and where is the largest mountain in Africa?
12. Name three African empires.
13. What country "gave birth" to Egypt?
14. What is the original name of Egypt?
15. What does Kemet mean?
16. Which Nubian King had the Step pyramid built?
17. Who was Imhotep and what did the Greeks call him?
18. What is the name of oldest & most noted statute carved from one rock?
19. Describe the Sphinx.
20. Name the four parts of the Sphinx.
21. Who was the Kemetic King to start the first dynasty in Kemet?

22. Which Kemetic Queen ruled as a Pharoah?
23. What are the measurements of the Great Pyramid
24. How much did each stone weigh and how many stones were used?
25. Which Kemetic King had the Great Pyramid built?
26. Name the three pyramids that are in the center of the earth.
27. Which Kemetic queen name means 'The Beautiful One has come'?
28. Which Kemetic King introduced the world to the belief in one God?
29. Who were King Tutenkamun's(Tut) parents?
30. What is the Kemetic style of writing called?
31. What does Metu Neter mean?
32. What are the seven virtues of Ma'at?
33. Which Kemetic deities are credited with teaching civilization to Kemet?
34. Which Kemetic deity is the brother of Ausar?
35. Which Kemetic deity is the wife of Ausar?
36. Which Kemetic Deity is the son of Ausar and Auset?
37. Which Mali king was known for 'The Great Caravan of Gold'?
38. What is the name of the ancient school built by Mansa Musa?
39. What was the name of the fierce warrior that established the Songhai Empire?
40. What's the name one of the first university?
41. Why was it called 'university'?
42. How many subjects were taught?

Kindergarten to 12th Grade Can = 13 Years A Slave

43. How many years were they in school?
44. What was the name of the group of Africans that helped to civilize Europe?
45. How long did the Moors rule Spain?
46. Who were the first civilized white people?
47. Name the first five invaders of Africa.
48. Five things Black people couldn't do during slavery.
49. Five things Black people did to resist slavery.
50. Is slavery African History?

APPENDIX B
Suggested Reading Books & Authors

Nile Valley Contributions to Civilization(Exploding the Myths)
The Browder Files: 22 Essays on the African American Experience
    by Anthony T. Browder

Destruction of Black Civilization
    by Chancellor Williams

The New Jim Crow: Mass Incarceration in the Age of Colorblindness
    by Michelle Alexander

Lies My Teacher Told Me
    by James Loewen

The Philosophy and Opinions of Marcus Garvey, Or, Africa for the Africans
    by Marcus Garvey

The Autobiography of Malcolm X
    As Told to Alex Haley

The Spirit of a Man: A Vision of Transformation for Black Men and the Women Who Love Them
    by Iyanla Vanzant

Countering the Conspiracy to Destroy Black Boys Volumes I-IV
    by Jawanza Kunjufu

The Isis Papers: The Keys to the Colors
    by Dr. Frances Cress Welsing

Things Fall Apart
    by Chinua Achebe

Where Do We Go from Here: Chaos or Community? (King Legacy)
    by Dr. Martin Luther King Jr.

The Community of Self
Visions for Black Men
New Visions for Black Men
    by Na'im Akbar

Black-On-Black Violence: The Psychodynamics of Black Self-Annihilation in service of White Domination
Blueprint for Black Power: A Moral, Political and Economic Imperative for the Twenty-First Century
    by Amos N. Wilson

The Mis-Education of the Negro
    by Carter G. Woodson

PowerNomics: The National Plan to Empower Black America
Black Labor, White Wealth: The Search for Power and Economic Justice
    by Dr. Claud Anderson

I Write What I Like: Selected Writings
    by Steve Biko

How Europe Underdeveloped Africa
    by Walter Rodney

Black Skin, White Masks
    by Frantz Fanon

Rickie Clark

Africa Must Unite
    by Kwame Nkrumah

The African Origin of Civilization: Myth or Reality
    by Cheikh Anta Diop

Negro with a Hat: The Rise and Fall of Marcus Garvey
    by Colin Grant

Introduction to Maat Philosophy: spiritual Enlightment Through the Path of Righteous Action
    by Muata Ashby

They Came Before Columbus: The African Presence in Ancient America (Journal of African Civilizations)
    by Ivan Van Sertima

Stolen Legacy: with Illustrations
    by George G. M. James

To Die for the People
    by Huey Newton

Breaking the Curse of Willie Lynch: The Science of Slave Psychology
    by Alvin Morrow

Assata: An Autobiography
    by Assata Shakur and Angela Davis

Black Genesis: The Prehistoric Origins of Ancient Egypt
    by Robert Bauval and Thomas Brophy PhD.

The Journey of the Songhai People

Pan African Federation Organization collection of books of this topic
> by Calvin Robinson, Redman Battle & Edward Robinson

African Pyramids of Knowledge
> by Molefi Kete Asante

Cointelpro: The FBI's Secret War on Political Freedom
> by Nelson Blackstock

APPENDIX C
Suggested Movies

12 Years a Slave
Hidden Colors 1, 2, and 3
Hidden Figures
Mississippi Burning
The Butler
Django Unchained
Get Out
Glory
Fruitvale Station
Hotel Rowanda
Roots
Cry Freedom
Sankofa
A Time to Kill
Life
Rosewood
Black Panther
The Great Debaters
Amistad
The Tuskegee Airmen
Blood Diamonds
Higher Learning
Do the Right Thing

The Help
In the Heat of the Night
A Soldier Story
Malcolm X
School Daze
Jungle Fever
Imitation of Life
Claudine
Get on the Bus
The Long Walk Home
Red Tails
Miss Evers' Boys
1915: Birth of a Nation
Nat Turner Story
Coming to America
Bamboozled
Straight Outta Compton
Boyz n the Hood
The Color Purple
Imitation of Life

APPENDIX D
Suggested Documentaries

Chaka Zulu

Four Little Girls

The Untold Story of Emmett Till

The Jackie Robinson Story

Eyes on the Prize

Tuskegee Airmen

The Rosa Parks Story

What Happen Miss Simone?

Slavery by Another Name

Freedom Riders

Black Power Mixed Tape 1967- 1975

The 13th

Martin Luther King Jr. American Dream

Martin Luther King Jr. American Nightmare

Black Panther's: Vanguard of Revolution

Fredrick Douglas and the White Negro

Maafa 21

Marcus Garvey: Look for Me in the Worldwind

Marian Anderson: The Lincoln Memorial Concert

The Murder of Fred Hampton

The Haitian Revolution 180

British Slave Trade

Sam Cooke

W. E. B. DuBois

Paul Robeso

APPENDIX E
50 Questions Key Answers

1. Alkebulan
2. Africa
3. Continent
4. 55
5. Three times larger
6. Africa
7. Kenya, female
8. Diamonds, Gold, Colton
9. Madagascar, Tanzania, Egypt, Ghana and Kenya
10. Nile River
11. Mount Kilamanjaro, which is in Tanzania
12. Songhai, Mali and Ghana
13. Nubia
14. Kemet
15. The Land of the Black people
16. King Djoser
17. The world's first known multi-genius, Asklepios (God of Medicine)
18. The Sphinx
19. The body of a lion and the head of a human.
20. Man, beast, brain and body
21. King Narmer
22. Queen Hatshepsut
23. 48 stories high and 755 feet wide
24. Each stone weighed two tons or more and it took 2,300,000 stones to build it.

25. King Kfufu

26. Kfufu, Khafra and Menkaure

27. Queen Nefertiti

28. King Akhenaten

29. Queen Nafertiti (step-mother) and King Akhenaten, father

30. Hieroglyphics

31. Writing of the Gods

32. Truth, Justice, Harmony, Balance, Order, Reciprocity, and Propriety

33. Osiris

34. Set

35. Isis

36. Horus

37. Mansa Musa

38. Timbuktu

39. Sonni Ali

40. Luxor

41. Because they had studied the universe

42. Four

43. 40 years

44. Moors

45. 800 years

46. Greeks

47. Name the first five invaders of Africa.

48. They couldn't: read & write, play drums, be in groups of five or more, own fire arms, have church without a white person in the audience
49. To resist they would: poison slave owners, break tools, burn buildings, have deliberate work slow-downs
50. No, it's an interruption of African History.

About The Author, Rickie Clark

No one defies stereotypes, generalizations or clichés more than Rickie Clark. Growing up poor in Chicago, Illinois, raised by a single mother on the south side; Rickie was told by a high school teacher that he was not "college material". Fortunately, there was another teacher who believed he was destined for more.

Rickie currently serves as a Consultant for the My Brother's Keeper Program (MBK) in the Fort Worth Independent School District(FWISD). This initiative of former President Barack Obama, mentors young men of color as they transition from one life stage to another. Mr. Clark has a career spanning over 30 years, affecting real change in the lives of youth.

He is an Educational Consultant and Advocate for the Tarrant County Youth Advocate Program and a motivational speaker. He is a Trainer of Trainers for Violence Intervention and Prevention, Youth Entrepreneurship and Rites of Passage programs. He is also the author of the book, *What My Daddy Should Have Told Me: Life Lessons for the African-American Male.*

Clark is a 1983 graduate of Jarvis Christian College. He has been instrumental in helping many youth that society has given up on with ways for them to recognize and achieve their greater potential. He embraces the philosophy, 'in order to be a man, you must see a man.'

Clark travels throughout the United States designing, teaching and implementing programs for young men of color.

How to Work with Rickie Clark

Rickie Clark goes one step beyond traditional practices to equip young men with sustainable knowledge and skills that they can retain for a life time. Clark is a gifted communicator who offers encouragement, motivation, and inspiration to all those who come onto his path. His genuine transparency comes through in the examples he gives his audiences as he guides them to manhood intentionally, consciously and purposefully. Clark conducts trainings and workshops for colleges, school districts, community and faith-based organizations.

For more information about working with Rickie Clark:
Email: info@rickieclark.com
Website: www.rickieclark.com

Made in the USA
Middletown, DE
20 October 2022

13152977R00057